I'm Ready To Learn About
BEGINNING READING

by
Imogene Forte

Illustrated by Gayle Seaberg Harvey
Cover illustration by Francis Huffman
Edited by Jennifer Goodman

ISBN 0-86530-110-7
Copyright © 1986 by Incentive Publications, Inc., Nashville, TN. All rights reserved. Permission is hereby granted to the purchaser of one copy of I'M READY TO LEARN ABOUT BEGINNING READING to reproduce pages in sufficient quantity to meet needs of students in one classroom or for children in one household.

TO PARENTS AND TEACHERS

Why You Need This Book

- The READY TO LEARN SERIES capitalizes on the vitally important "teachable" years from 3-5.
- Basic skills and concepts are introduced to help pave the way to increased self-confidence and lifelong learning success.

What Children Will Learn From This Book

- Children will develop the following basic beginning reading skills.
  - Visual discrimination
  - Letter recognition
  - Letter discrimination
  - Letter/sound recognition
  - Recognizing and using rhyming words, easy words and descriptive words
  - Associating words and pictures
  - Recognizing words by configuration
  - Ordering ideas in sequence
  - Classifying
  - Visualizing
  - Following directions
  - Finding the main idea

How To Get The Most From This Book

- Read and interpret the directions for your child.
- Keep the atmosphere light and relaxed.
- Allow the child to work at his or her own pace, free from pressure to perform.
- Praise the child's efforts!

BONUS

See the suggested activities at the back of this book to extend and reinforce the skills and concepts learned.

---

is ready to learn about
BEGINNING READING

Do you know your color words?
Color the balloons.

Recognizing and using color words
©1986 by Incentive Publications, Inc., Nashville, TN.

The drummer has a **red drum.**
Color the drum.

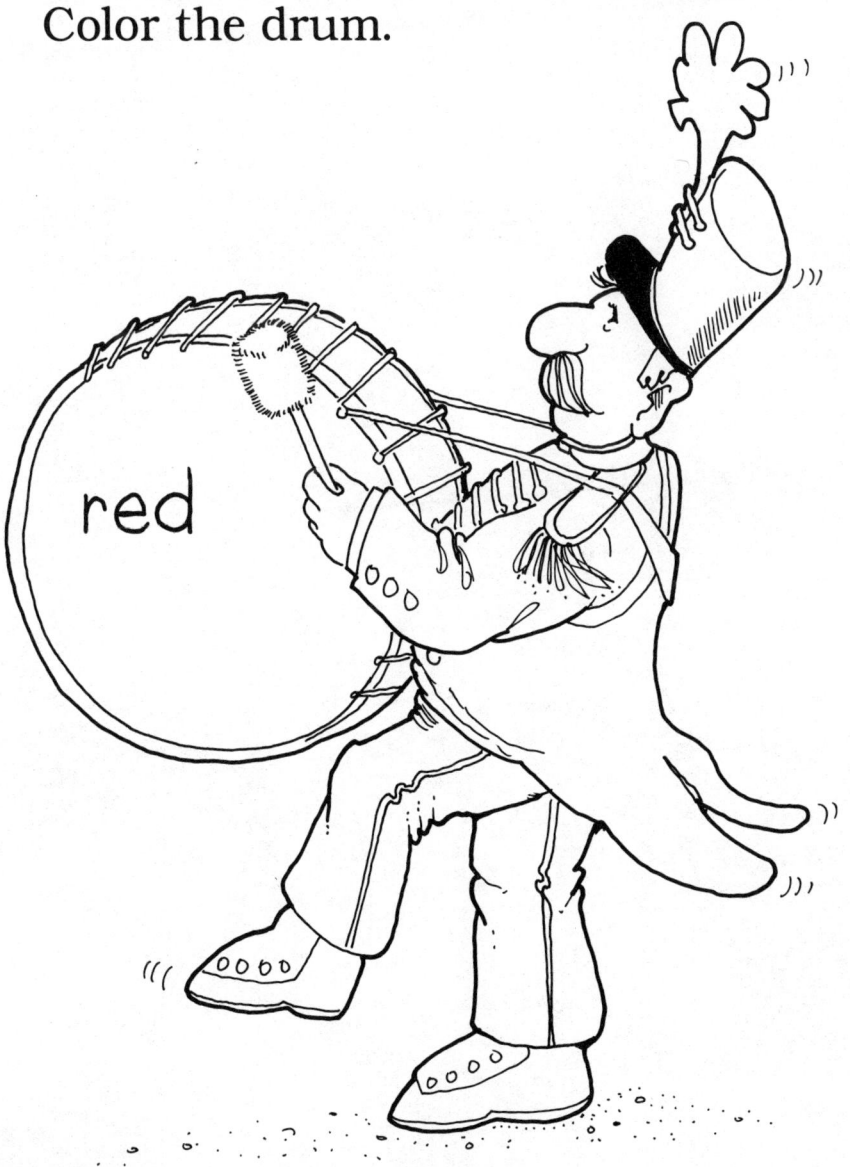

Word recognition
©1986 by Incentive Publications, Inc., Nashville, TN.

Color each balloon.

Identifying color words
©1986 by Incentive Publications, Inc., Nashville, TN.

Draw lines to match the letters and the picture whose name begins with that letter.

Letter/sound recognition
©1986 by Incentive Publications, Inc., Nashville, TN.

Draw lines to match the letters and the picture whose name begins with that letter.

Circle the hat in each row that is different.
Color all the hats.

Visual discrimination/finding differences

Something is wrong. Color everything except the mistakes.

Visual discrimination/finding mistakes
©1986 by Incentive Publications, Inc., Nashville, TN.

Cut and paste the words in the correct spaces.

Oh my,
Oh me,
I see the

☐

A big, fat cat
Wore a big,
black

☐

| hat | bee |

Recognizing and using rhyming words
©1986 by Incentive Publications, Inc., Nashville, TN.

Match the lower case letters with the capital letters.

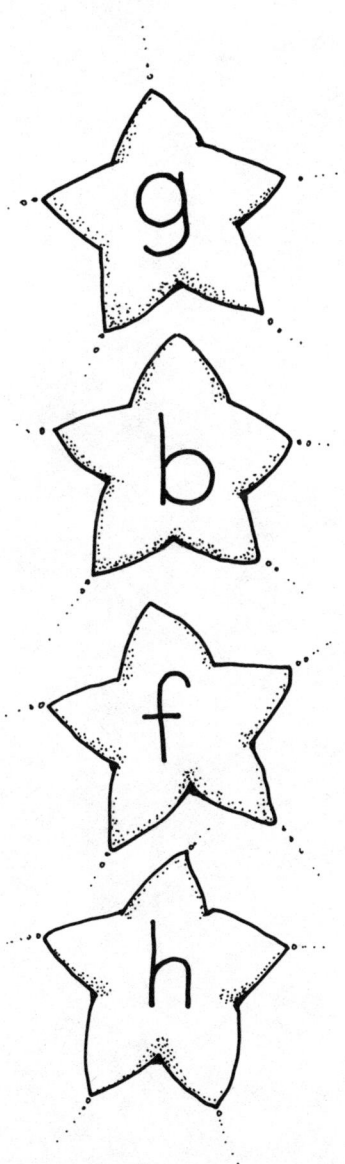
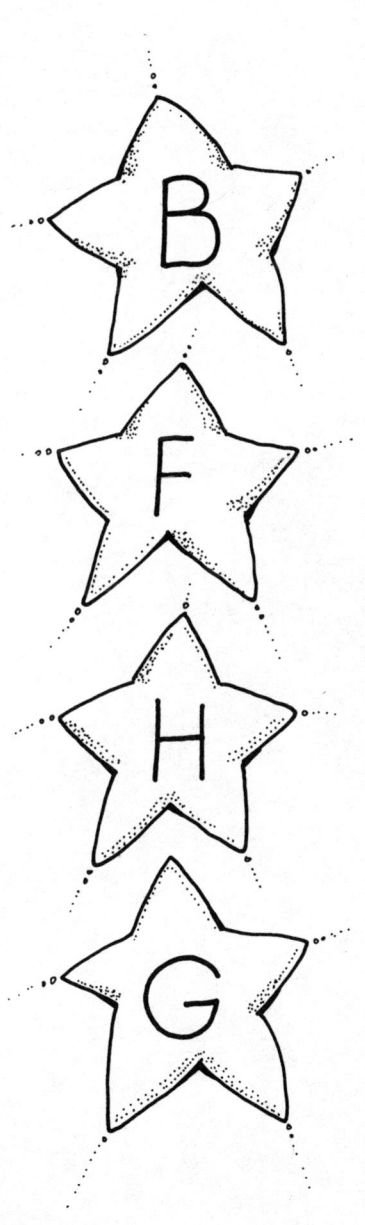

Discriminating upper and lower case letters
©1986 by Incentive Publications, Inc., Nashville, TN.

To join the parade, draw dot-to-dot from A to Z.

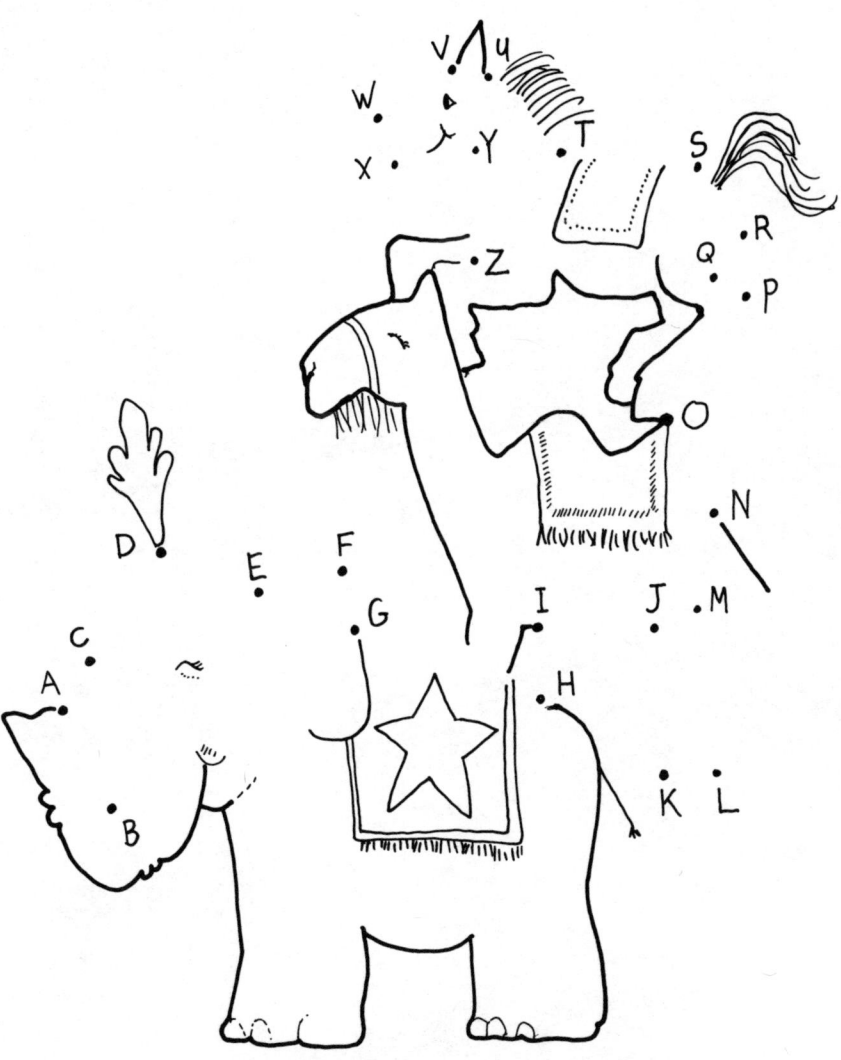

Letter recognition
©1986 by Incentive Publications, Inc., Nashville, TN.

Winkie the clown likes to play ball.
Circle the word ball.

Recognizing words by configuration

Cut and paste the words in the correct boxes.
Say the words.

Recognizing and using descriptive words
©1986 by Incentive Publications, Inc., Nashville, TN.

Rain, rain go away,
Come again another day;
Johnny wants to play.

Number the pictures in order 1, 2 and 3.

Ordering ideas in sequence
©1986 by Incentive Publications, Inc., Nashville, TN.

Cut and paste the letter b on each picture whose name begins like ball.

Recognizing initial consonant sounds
©1986 by Incentive Publications, Inc., Nashville, TN.

Draw a line to connect the things that belong together.

Understanding relationships
©1986 by Incentive Publications, Inc., Nashville, TN.

Chucko is a happy clown.
He has a big nose and a round mouth.
He wears funny clothes.
Draw Chucko.

Visualizing
©1986 by Incentive Publications, Inc., Nashville, TN.

Color the big lion yellow.
Color the small lion orange.
Color the lion tamer's shoes black.

Following directions
©1986 by Incentive Publications, Inc., Nashville, TN.

Cut and paste the words that end with the same sound as monkey.

| key | donkey | tiger |

Recognizing vowel sounds
©1986 by Incentive Publications, Inc., Nashville, TN.

Match the words to the pictures.
Color the pictures.

tree

sun

dog

Associating words and pictures
©1986 by Incentive Publications, Inc., Nashville, TN.

Color the spaces with lower case letters red.
Color the spaces with capital letters yellow.

Discriminating upper and lower case letters
©1986 by Incentive Publications, Inc., Nashville, TN.

Find four dancing dogs.
Color each dog a different color.

Visual discrimination/hidden pictures
©1986 by Incentive Publications, Inc., Nashville, TN.

Find four dancing dogs.
Color each dog a different color.

Say the names of the pictures.
Match the rhyming pictures.

Matching rhyming pictures
©1986 by Incentive Publications, Inc., Nashville, TN.

Color the animals.

Classifying
©1986 by Incentive Publications, Inc., Nashville, TN.

Cut and paste the pictures beside the words.

hat

bed

Associating words and pictures
©1986 by Incentive Publications, Inc., Nashville, TN.

All the capital letters are hiding in this picture.
Find and color all 26 letters.

Recognizing capital letters
©1986 by Incentive Publications, Inc., Nashville, TN.

Draw a line from the numeral to the number word.

1 — three
2 — one
3 — two
4 — four

Recognizing number words
©1986 by Incentive Publications, Inc., Nashville, TN.

Trace over the dotted lines.
Circle the sentence that goes with the picture.

Here is a dog.

Here is a tree.

Finding the main idea
©1986 by Incentive Publications, Inc., Nashville, TN.

Circle the clown twins that are exactly alike.
Color the other clowns.

Visual discrimination/matching
©1986 by Incentive Publications, Inc., Nashville, TN.

Help the ringmaster get into the ring.
Draw a line to show the way.

Visual discrimination/maze
©1986 by Incentive Publications, Inc., Nashville, TN.

Help the ringmaster get into the ring
Draw a line to show the way.

EVERYDAY ACTIVITIES AND PROJECTS FOR CHILDREN
Ready to Learn About Beginning Reading

- Place simple geometric shapes on a table. Have the child pick out the shapes that are the same size, shape or color.
- Choose a can of food. Give it to the child and let him select an identical can from the pantry.
- Invest in two identical magazines. Cut out brightly colored pictures from one. Have the child find and cut out the same pictures from the other magazine.
- Choose a word such as "goat" and ask the child to tell you some rhyming words.
- Strengthen sequential memory through repetition. Clap your hands using a distinct pattern. Ask the child to reproduce the pattern.
- Ask the child to name words which share the same beginning sound, i.e. ball (boat, big, etc.).
- Give the child sample sentences to repeat, such as:
  —Jerry reads books about knights and dragons.
  —April plays games and reads books.
  —Grandmother knitted a sweater that was red, blue and pink.
- Provide lots of good books and make reading a regular part of your family life style. Plan regular trips to the library and read-aloud sessions.
- Have the child practice tracing around household objects such as cans, spoons, square plastic containers, keys, recipe cards or scissors. Make a dotted pattern of these items on a piece of paper. The child may then follow and trace over these dotted patterns.